big NATE

A GOOD OLD-FASHIONED WEDGIE

More

adventures from

LINCOLN PEIRCE

Big Nate From the Top

Big Nate Out Loud

Big Nate and Friends

Big Nate Makes the Grade

Big Nate All Work and No Play

Big Nate: Game On!

Big Nate: I Can't Take It!

Big Nate: Great Minds Think Alike

Big Nate: The Crowd Goes Wild!

Big Nate's Greatest Hits

Big Nate: Say Good-bye to Dork City

Big Nate: Welcome to My World

Big Nate: Thunka, Thunka, Thunka

Big Nate: Revenge of the Cream Puffs

Epic Big Nate

Big Nate: What's a Little Noogie Between Friends?

big NATE

A GOOD OLD-FASHIONED WEDGIE

by LINCOLN PEIRCE

COME ON, CHESTER! HE'S NO BATTER! LET HIM HIT IT! IT WON'T MATTER!

THERE'S ANOTHER SWING AND MISS! HE CAN'T HIT! IT'S OBVIOUS!

LET'S GO, CHESTER! MOW HIM DOWN! THIS KID LOOKS LIKE SUCH A **CLOWN**!

I THINK THAT I SHALL NEVER SEE THIS DOOFUS HIT THE BALL TO ME!

SEE THAT SWING? THIS GUY'S A **DORK**! HE'S SO—

I'VE NEVER SEEN ANYONE BENCHED FOR POETRY BEFORE!
IT'S JUST AS WELL. I DIDN'T HAVE A RHYME FOR "DORK."

HEY! SINCE WHEN ARE STAN AND MICHELLE A COUPLE?
SINCE SHE LEFT AN "I LIKE YOU" NOTE IN HIS LOCKER.

HMPH! NOBODY EVER LEAVES AN "I LIKE YOU" NOTE IN **MY** LOCKER.

KSSSCHH!

I WONDER WHY.
WAIT, IS **THAT** ONE?
Peirce

AH **HA!** IT LOOKS LIKE SOMEBODY **DID** LEAVE A NOTE IN MY LOCKER!

"NATE - YOU ARE AWESOME, AMAZING, AND TOTALLY HOT."
WOW! THAT'S...

OH, WAIT A SEC. **I** WROTE THIS.

NEVER MIND.
HE FEELS GOOD ABOUT HIMSELF.
Peirce

WHY SHOULD I WAIT FOR SOME GIRL TO WRITE A NOTE TO ME? I'M WRITING A NOTE TO HER!

"DEAR HONEY CAKES: YOU ARE THE MOST INCREDIBLE GIRL ON THE PLANET. THE TWO OF US ARE DESTINED TO BE SOUL MATES."

WOW. WHO'S IT FOR?
I'M NOT SURE YET.

THAT'S SORT OF A KEY PART, DON'T YOU THINK?
NOT NECESSARILY. WHY LIMIT MY OPTIONS?
Peirce

WHAT'S THIS? THERE'S A **NOTE** IN MY LOCKER! FROM A **SECRET ADMIRER**!

IT SAYS THAT I'M THE SINGLE MOST FASCINATING GIRL IN THE WHOLE SCHOOL!
WOW! RUBY, THAT'S...

WAIT A MINUTE.

I GOT THE SAME NOTE.
HELLO, **LADIES**!
Peirce

?
AH! KATE! I SEE YOU GOT MY NOTE!

YOU WROTE THIS?
YUP! I'M JUST TESTING THE WATERS TO SEE IF A **ROMANCE** MIGHT BLOOM BETWEEN US!
ROWR!

WHAT DO YOU THINK? YES OR NO?

YOU'RE AN IDIOT.
I'LL PUT "MAYBE."
Peirce

HOW GOES THE SEARCH FOR ROMANCE?
PRETTY GOOD. I'VE RECEIVED THREE RESPONSES TO MY NOTES.

MARY CALLED ME AN IMBECILE, KATE CALLED ME AN IDIOT, AND CARRIE CALLED ME A MORON.

I DID SOME RESEARCH, AND I FOUND OUT THAT A MORON IS SMARTER THAN AN IMBECILE, AND AN IMBECILE IS SMARTER THAN AN IDIOT.

SO: CARRIE IT IS!
SHE'LL BE SO EXCITED.
Peirce

HEH HEH! THAT MOVIE LOOKS GOOD!

GRUMBLE BUT OF COURSE IT'S RATED R!
BEING ELEVEN STINKS. I WISH I WAS OLDER.
YUP. WHEN YOU'RE OLDER, YOU CAN GO TO ANY MOVIE YOU WANT.

YOU CAN DO ANYTHING! COOK YOUR OWN MEALS, DO YOUR OWN LAUNDRY... ANYTHING!

EVEN BETTER: YOU DON'T HAVE TO GO TO SCHOOL FOR 30 HOURS EVERY WEEK! YOU GET YOURSELF A JOB AND WORK 60 HOURS!

AND AFTER YOU GET FIRED FIVE MONTHS BEFORE YOUR PENSION KICKS IN, YOU CAN START A WHOLE NEW, EXCITING CAREER AT AGE 62!

WHY RETIRE? YOU CAN KEEP WORKING UNTIL YOU HAVE A NEAR-FATAL HEART ATTACK!

OOP. THAT REMINDS ME. I NEED TO TAKE MY PILLS.

SUNNY DAY... SWEEPIN' THE CLOUDS AWAY...
Peirce

... SO EVEN THOUGH WE GOT THERE LATE, WE DECIDED TO SEE THE MOVIE IRREGARDLESS.
NO. NO. NO.

WHAT?
YOU CAN'T SAY "IRREGARDLESS"! THERE IS NO SUCH WORD!

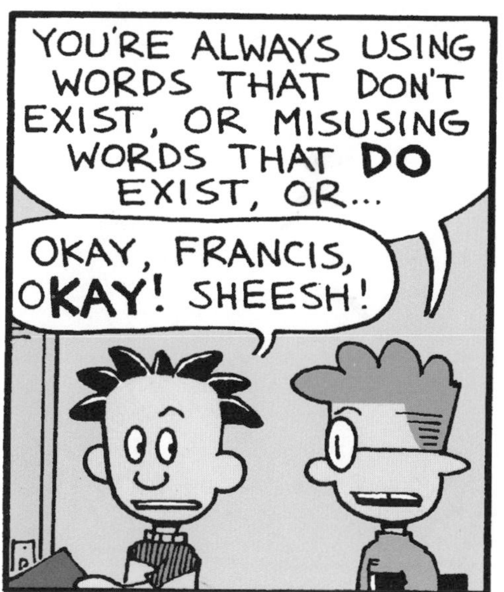
YOU'RE ALWAYS USING WORDS THAT DON'T EXIST, OR MISUSING WORDS THAT DO EXIST, OR...
OKAY, FRANCIS, OKAY! SHEESH!

ANYWAY, THE MOVIE WAS TOTALLY ANTICLIMATIC.
NO. NO! NO!
Peirce

IT'S GETTING LATE. I'M GONNA HEAD TOWARDS HOME.
NOT "TOWARDS."

HM?
THERE'S NO "S." IT'S TOWARD, NOT TOWARDS.

WHAT-EVER.
"WHATEVER"? DOESN'T IT BOTHER YOU WHEN PEOPLE USE THE WRONG WORD?

I COULD CARE LESS.
CRIPES.
Peirce

I'M BEAT. I NEED TO LAY DOWN.
NO! YOU DON'T **LAY** DOWN, YOU **LIE** DOWN!

YOU USE "LAY" WHEN YOU **PUT** SOMETHING SOMEWHERE! YOU **LAY** A BLANKET ON THE GRASS! YOU **LAY** A PLATE ON A PLACEMAT! GET IT?
YEAH, I GET IT.

SO. YOU HAVE A BOOK. WHAT DO YOU DO WITH IT?

DOOF!
Peirce

YOU KNOW, FRANCIS, IT'S PRETTY ANNOYING WHEN YOU CORRECT WHAT I **SAY** ALL THE TIME!
I CAN'T HELP IT! IT'S MY PET PEEVE!

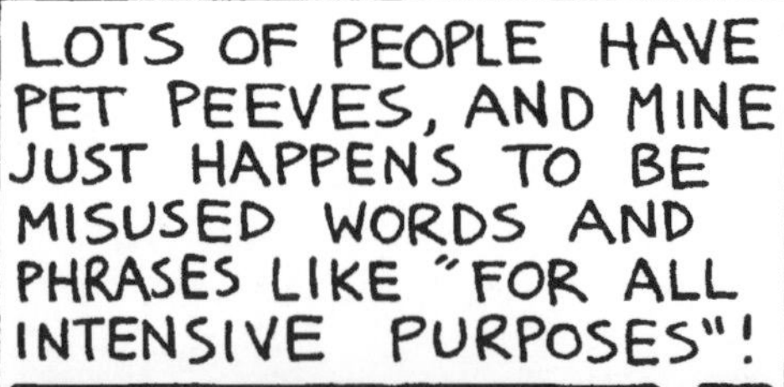
LOTS OF PEOPLE HAVE PET PEEVES, AND MINE JUST HAPPENS TO BE MISUSED WORDS AND PHRASES LIKE "FOR ALL INTENSIVE PURPOSES"!

DO **YOU** HAVE ANY PET PEEVES?
OH, YEAH, I'VE GOT MILLIONS OF 'EM...

...LITERALLY.
GAH!

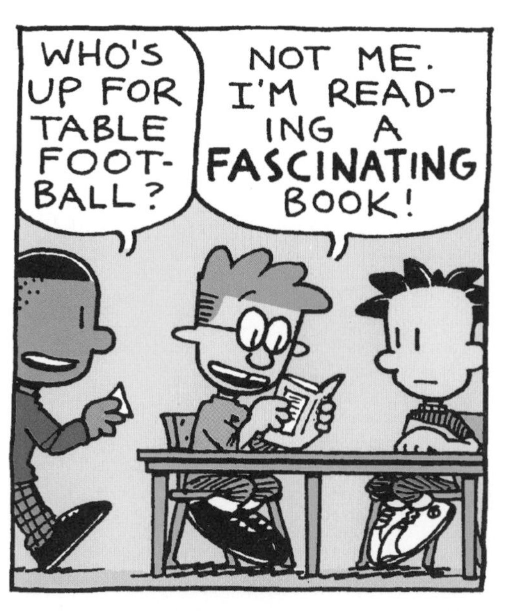
WHO'S UP FOR TABLE FOOT-BALL?
NOT ME. I'M READ-ING A **FASCINATING** BOOK!

IT'S CALLED "COMMONLY MISUSED WORDS AND PHRASES IN SPEECH AND LITERATURE."

MM-HM... UH-HUH... OH, THAT IS **SO** TRUE! OH, **YES!**... IT DRIVES ME **CRAZY** WHEN PEOPLE SAY THAT! OH, AMEN!... A**MEN!**... YES! OH, YES! **YES!**

I'M A LITTLE CREEPED OUT RIGHT NOW. JUST SAYIN'.
I'LL PLAY, BUT ONLY IF WE MOVE TO ANOTHER TABLE.

...AND SOLDIERS OFTEN RETURNED TO THE BATTLEFIELD TO LOOK FOR SOUVENIRS AND MOMENTOS.
MRS. GODFREY?

THAT'S A COMMON MISTAKE. THE WORD IS ACTUALLY **MEM**ENTO, NOT **MO**MENTO.

...BUT HOWEVER YOU WANT TO SAY IT IS FINE WITH ME.
THAT'S WHAT'S KNOWN AS A "HAIRY EYEBALL."
Peirce

SIGH...

MRS. CZERWICKI, WHY ARE WE HERE?

DETENTION IS A TOTALLY OUTDATED WAY OF PUNISHING STUDENTS!

WHAT GOOD DOES IT DO, MAKING US SIT HERE FOR AN HOUR DOING NOTHING?

MOST SCHOOLS DON'T EVEN HAVE DETENTION ANYMORE! THEY'VE FIGURED OUT HOW USELESS IT IS!

SO I ASK AGAIN: WHY ARE WE HERE?

I'M HERE BECAUSE IT'S MY JOB.
YOU'RE HERE BECAUSE YOU PLAYED "SURFIN' USA" WITH YOUR ARMPIT OVER THE INTERCOM.
SIT DOWN.

JUST FOR THE RECORD, IT WASN'T "SURFIN' USA," IT WAS "FUN, FUN, FUN."
HOW IRONIC.

GOOD MORNING, BOYS!
GOOD MORNING, MRS. GODFREY!
GRUNT

WELL, HELLO TO YOU TOO, NATE.

WHY DOES SHE ALWAYS SINGLE ME OUT?
Peirce

IF YOU WATCH THE WAY MRS. GODFREY TREATS ME, IT'S **TOTALLY** UNFAIR!

SHE'S ALWAYS YELLING AT ME! SHE'S ALWAYS SENDING ME TO DETENTION! NOT ANYBODY **ELSE**! JUST **ME**!

APPARENTLY THE FAT OLD COW HAS DECIDED SHE **HATES** ME FOR SOME REASON!

THE QUESTION IS: **WHY**?
Peirce

WHAT DID YOU JUST CALL ME, YOUNG MAN?
WHA-? ME? **NOTHING**! NOT A **THING**!

I WASN'T EVEN **TALKING**! I WAS.. *KOFF!*... I WAS **SINGING**! JUST... UH... PRACTICING A NEW **SONG**!

APPARENTLY THE FAT OLD COW HAS DECIDED SHE **HATES** ME FOR SOME REASON!
!

CATCHY LYRICS.
I AM SO DEAD.

REPORT TO DETENTION AFTER SCHOOL, NATE.

WHILE YOU'RE THERE, PERHAPS YOU CAN THINK ABOUT HOW **HURTFUL** NAME-CALLING CAN BE!

GOT IT?
UH-HUH.

LITTLE ████.

IF YOU WANT MRS. GODFREY TO BE NICE TO **YOU**, THEN YOU HAVE TO BE NICE TO—
THAT DOESN'T **WORK**, FRANCIS! I'VE **TRIED**!

RIGHT. YOU'VE TRIED.
I **HAVE**! JUST LAST MONTH! YOU SAW IT WITH YOUR OWN **EYES**!

I TRIED TO ENGAGE HER IN A FRIENDLY CONVERSATION, AND SHE TOTALLY **SHUT ME DOWN**!

PERHAPS BECAUSE THERE WAS AN EXAM GOING ON AT THE TIME.
WELL, IS THAT ANY EXCUSE FOR HER TO BE **RUDE**?

LET'S TAKE A POLL! FRANCIS, WHY DO YOU THINK MRS. GODFREY TREATS NATE THE WAY SHE DOES?

BECAUSE HE NEVER PAYS ATTENTION IN CLASS AND HE DOESN'T APPLY HIMSELF.
CHAD, WHAT DO **YOU** THINK?

"BECAUSE MRS. GODFREY IS A PSYCHOTIC GAS BAG."

THE CHADS HAVE IT!
I HAVE TRAINED YOU WELL, YOUNG JEDI!

...AND THE BAILEYS HAD A COUPLE OF BIKES STOLEN...
HM. THAT'S THE FOURTH BREAK-IN I'VE HEARD ABOUT.

I'M THINKING OF INVESTING IN A SECURITY SYSTEM.
NO NEED, MR. EUSTIS! I'VE GOT A CHEAPER WAY TO PROTECT YOUR PROPERTY!

A SIMPLE "BEWARE OF DOG" SIGN!
BEWARE OF DOG

DOGS PREVENT MORE BURGLARIES THAN SECURITY SYSTEMS DO! WE'LL JUST STICK THIS IN YOUR FRONT YARD, AND...
BEWARE OF DOG

'SCUSE ME A SEC.

YOU'RE GOING TO HAVE TO MOVE TO THE BACK OF THE HOUSE.

BAD NEWS, CREAM PUFFS. CHESTER HAD TO QUIT THE TEAM.
COACH
GROANN!

THAT STINKS! CHESTER'S OUR BEST PITCHER!
I WONDER WHY HE QUIT.

MAYBE PLAYING BASE-BALL VIOLATED THE TERMS OF HIS PAROLE!
HEH HEH!

ARE YOU MAKING FUN OF MY CUDDLE BUNNY?
NO, I WOULD NEVER MAKE FUN OF YOUR CUDDLE BUNNY.

KIM, WHY'D CHESTER QUIT THE TEAM?
HIS PARENTS MADE HIM.

THEY SAY THEY WANT HIM TO FOCUS ON HIS SCHOOLWORK, BUT **I** THINK THEY WANT TO KEEP HIM AWAY FROM **ME**.

THEY'RE AFRAID HE'S BECOME UTTERLY INTOXICATED BY MY FLIRTATIOUS, BUBBLY PERSONALITY.

I HAVE THAT EFFECT ON PEOPLE.
MUST... NOT... SAY... ANYTHING.

WHAT'LL WE DO WITHOUT CHESTER? HE'S OUR **ACE**!
WE'LL FIND A **NEW** ACE!

DAD, GREAT PITCHERS DON'T GROW ON **TREES**!
I KNOW...

...BUT I FEEL A BRILLIANT IDEA COMING ON!

IS IT A BETTER IDEA THAN OUR FAMILY VACATION TO "CAMP EVERFREE?"
HOW WAS **I** SUPPOSED TO KNOW IT WAS A NUDIST COLONY?

YOU STILL HAVEN'T TOLD ME HOW WE'RE GOING TO REPLACE CHESTER!
YOU'LL SEE!

WHOA, WAIT A MINUTE! IT'S ME, ISN'T IT? AS THE ASSISTANT COACH, YOU CAN MAKE ME OUR STAR PITCHER!

I WOULDN'T DO THAT, NATE. THAT WOULD BE NEPOTISM.
WHAT?

BUT WE'RE FAMILY!
NEVER-THELESS...

DAD, WHY ARE YOU BEING ALL **MYSTERIOUS**?
ABOUT WHAT?

AARRGH! JUST TELL ME WHO'S GOING TO TAKE CHESTER'S PLACE ON THE TEAM!!

DING DONG!

WHY DON'T YOU ANSWER THE DOOR AND FIND OUT?
?

DING DONG!
GET THE DOOR, NATE.

WHO IS IT? IS IT OUR NEW PITCHER?
THAT'S A POSSI-BILITY.

!

REMEMBER ME?

WHAT'S UP, MIRANDA?
HAVE YOU SEEN MY DOLL?

NOPE, DON'T THINK SO.
I LEFT HER ON MY PORCH, AND NOW SHE'S GONE!

HOW WILL I FIND HER?
I KNOW!

DOGS HAVE SUPER SENSITIVE NOSES! WE'LL TRACK DOWN YOUR DOLL BY USING A DOG!

YOU HAVE A DOG?
NO, BUT MY NEIGHBOR DOES! C'MON!

SPITSY'S SENSE OF SMELL IS AMAZING! HE'LL FIND YOUR DOLL IN NO TIME!

!

HEY!
SPITSY, YOU IDIOT.

NATE, YOU KNOW LILA!
LILA?... UH... WAIT, DO I KNOW YOU FROM SCHOOL?

NO, I GO TO SAINT PAT'S.
BUT THE TWO OF YOU **USED** TO BE SCHOOL FRIENDS!

WE WENT TO PRE-K TOGETHER.
WE DID?

I USED TO BEAT YOU UP EVERY DAY DURING STORY TIME.
THAT WAS **YOU**?

SO, LILA... UH... YOU'RE A PITCHER?
YUP! I HEAR YOUR TEAM NEEDS ONE!

WANNA PLAY CATCH? I'LL SHOW YOU MY KILLER CHANGE-UP!
SURE! LET'S DO IT!

YOU NEED YOUR GLOVE.
RIGHT.

IT'S FUNNY WE WENT TO PRE-K TOGETHER!
AND AFTER THAT, YOU WENT TO SAINT PAT'S?

NOT AT FIRST. MY FOLKS HOME-SCHOOLED ME FOR TWO YEARS.
WOW! LILA! YOU WERE HOME-SCHOOLED?

I CAN'T IMAGINE BEING HOME-SCHOOLED! I MEAN, FOR ME THAT WOULD BE A TOTAL...

...LY DELIGHTFUL EXPERIENCE.
UH-HUH.

I WORK WITH YOUR DAD, LILA, AND HE SAYS YOU'RE QUITE A BALLPLAYER!
I'M OKAY!

MY FIELDING AND HITTING NEED A LITTLE WORK...

...BUT WAIT 'TIL YOU SEE MY FASTBALL! I'VE GOT A REALLY GOOD ARM!

THE REST OF HER'S NOT TOO SHABBY EITHER.
EASY, SLUGGER.

OKAY, LILA! SHOW ME WHAT YOU'VE GOT!

COMIN' ATCHA!
ZING!

WUMP!
OOF!

NATE?
WOWZA!

WOW! LILA! YOU THROW ALMOST AS HARD AS **CHESTER!**

SO YOU THINK I CAN HELP YOUR TEAM?
DEFINITELY! STARTING TOMORROW AGAINST AL'S AUTO GLASS!

I COULD... UH... COME BY YOUR HOUSE AT THREE, AND WE COULD WALK TO THE GAME... Y'KNOW... TOGETHER.
SURE!

...OR I COULD DRIVE ALL OF US TO THE GAME!
... OR YOU COULD MEET US **AT THE FIELD!**

PETER, M'BOY!
GREETINGSH!

WHAT'S UP?
REMEMBER LASHT WINTER WHEN WE LURED YOUR FRIENDSH INTO A SHNOWBALL AMBUSH?

DO I EVER! TEDDY AND FRANCIS ARE SUCH SUCKERS!
CAN WE DO THAT AGAIN? THAT WASH FUN!

SURE! I'M ALWAYS UP FOR AN AMBUSH!
AWESHOME!

THE QUESTION IS: WHERE DO WE SPRING THE TRAP?
HOW ABOUT YOUR SHED? IT WORKED LASHT TIME!

BUT WE CAN'T NAIL 'EM WITH SNOWBALLS, OBVIOUSLY! WHAT'LL WE HIT 'EM WITH?

SLAM!

WE'LL THINK OF SHOME-THING!
EASY AS PIE!

HI, LILA!
HI, NATE! READY FOR THE GAME?

YEAH! WITH YOU ON THE MOUND, AL'S AUTO GLASS HAS NO CHANCE!
I STILL THINK THIS IS A RIOT, DON'T YOU?

WE GO TO PRESCHOOL TOGETHER... THEN WE DON'T SEE EACH OTHER FOR SEVEN YEARS... AND NOW WE'RE ON THE SAME BASEBALL TEAM!
I KNOW!

WE HAVE SO MUCH IN COMMON!
Peirce

COACH, HERE'S LILA, THE YOUNG LADY I TOLD YOU ABOUT!
HI, LILA! WELCOME TO THE CREAM PUFFS!

I UNDERSTAND FROM MR. WRIGHT THAT YOU THROW RIGHTY, BAT LEFTY, AND LIKE TO PLAY THE OUTFIELD WHEN YOU'RE NOT PITCHING!
RIGHT!
COACH
Peirce

ANYTHING ELSE I SHOULD KNOW?

AHEM! SHE AND I WERE QUITE CLOSE IN PRE-SCHOOL.
THANK YOU, NATE. THAT'S VERY HELPFUL.

GUYS, THIS IS LILA, OUR NEW PITCHER! LILA, MEET TEDDY AND FRANCIS!
HI!

...AND THIS IS KIM!
H'LO.
Peirce

I'M GLAD THERE'S ANOTHER GIRL JOINING THE TEAM.

IT'S BEEN A BURDEN BEING THE ONLY BOMBSHELL.
OOH! CAN I BE A BOMB-SHELL?

STRIKE THREE!!

WOW! LILA STRUCK OUT THE SIDE!...
UH-OH. I'VE SEEN THAT LOOK.
WHAT LOOK?
Peirce

THAT LOVESTRUCK LOOK.
WHAT LOVESTRUCK LOOK?

THE ONE ON YOUR **FACE**!
WHAT FACE?

GREAT PITCHING, LILA! YOU'RE MOWING 'EM DOWN!
CLAP!
THANKS, NATE!
CLAP!
CLAP!

LISTEN TO THAT CROWD! YOU'VE GOT 'EM ALL FIRED UP!
CLAP!
CLAP!
CLAP!
CLAP!
CLAP!
CLAP!
CLAP!
CLAP!

WHO'S THE KID WHO WON'T STOP CLAPPING?
THAT'S MY BOY-FRIEND.
Peirce

OH.
ISN'T HE ADORABLE?

SO YOU...UH...YOU HAVE A BOYFRIEND. THAT'S GREAT, LILA. THAT'S... *KOFF!*... REALLY GREAT.
YEAH, HE'S AWESOME.

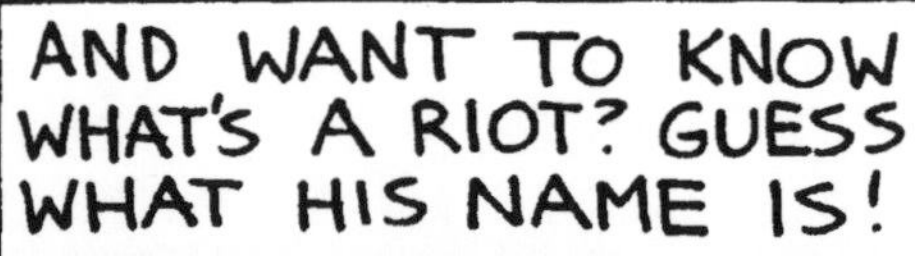
AND WANT TO KNOW WHAT'S A RIOT? GUESS WHAT HIS NAME IS!

IT'S **NATE!** ISN'T THAT FUNNY?
Peirce

HILARIOUS.

HEY, BOBBY.
HI, NATE. WANNA GO OVER TO...
WOOF
WORF

YIKES. WHO'S **THAT?**
OH, THAT'S JUST SPITSY.

HE SOUNDS LIKE A FIERCE ONE.
ARE YOU KIDDING? HE'S A WUSS.
WOOF
GRRF!
WORF!

WHO'S HE BARKING AT, THEN? ANOTHER DOG?
I DOUBT IT. LET'S CHECK IT OUT.

SEE? HE'S ATTACKING A **BUTTERFLY!**
ARF

WOW. NOW I'VE SEEN EVERYTHING.
ARF
WORF

DOOF!

NO, **NOW** I'VE SEEN EVERYTHING.
SPITSY, THIS IS A NEW LOW.
Peirce

SO LILA HAS A BOYFRIEND! WHAT A FOOL I AM! WHAT AN **IDIOT**!

I THOUGHT MAYBE SHE **LIKED** ME! HA! TO HER, I'M **NOBODY**! I'M JUST THE STINKIN' **RIGHT FIELDER**!

I BET STUFF LIKE THIS NEVER HAPPENS TO SHORTSTOPS.
Peirce

HOW COME ALL THE GIRLS WHO ARE **PER-FECT** FOR ME ALREADY **HAVE** BOYFRIENDS?

LILA AND I WERE GETTING ALONG **GREAT**! SHE WAS THE FIRST GIRL WHO MADE ME FORGET ABOUT...

ABOUT...

...JENNY??
Peirce

WHA-?... IS THAT... IS THAT **JENNY** OVER THERE?
!
!

IT'S **IMPOSSIBLE**!! SHE MOVED TO **SEATTLE**! COULD SHE BE **BACK**?

I CAN'T TELL... SHE'S STANDING BEHIND SOME PEOPLE... COME ON, LADY, MOVE OUT OF THE WAY SO I...

TONG!
peirce

WHAT HAPPENED?
NATE TOOK A FLY BALL RIGHT IN THE HEAD!

NATE! YOU OKAY?
GROAN...

JENNY...

HE'S DELUSIONAL!
TELL ME SOMETHING I DIDN'T KNOW.
SHUT UP.

I THINK YOU'LL BE OKAY. BUT YOU'VE GOT TO KEEP YOUR EYE ON THE BALL, CHAMP.
I KNOW...

...BUT I WASN'T SPACING OUT FOR NO REASON! I WAS **DISTRACTED** BY SOMETHING! BY SOME**ONE**!

BUT IT COULDN'T HAVE BEEN WHO I **THOUGHT** IT WAS, BECAUSE SHE **MOVED AWAY**!

...AND IN THE PROCESS, **RIPPED MY HEART OUT**!
BASEBALL AND ROMANCE DON'T MIX.
ACH

I DUNNO, IT WAS WEIRD. I LOOKED OVER AT THE CROWD, AND FOR A SPLIT SECOND I THOUGHT I SAW...

BETTER HURRY, KIDS! YOU'LL BE LATE FOR CLASS!

DON'T YOU WISH YOU WENT TO PRIVATE SCHOOL LIKE I DO?

MY SCHOOL YEAR'S OVER ALREADY! IT ENDED THREE DAYS AGO!

NOT ONLY THAT, WE DON'T HAVE TO MAKE UP SNOW DAYS LIKE PUBLIC SCHOOL KIDS!

AND WE DON'T WALK TO SCHOOL, EITHER! WE'RE DRIVEN THERE IN AN AIR-CONDITIONED BUS!

YANK!

AND YET, DESPITE ALL YOUR ADVANTAGES, YOU CAN'T FIND UNDERWEAR THAT FITS.

NOTHING ENDS AN UNPLEASANT CONVERSATION LIKE A GOOD OLD-FASHIONED WEDGIE!
I LIKE WALKING TO SCHOOL!
Peirce

JENNY! YOU'RE BACK FROM SEATTLE!
YUP!

SO... YOUR MOM QUIT HER JOB OUT THERE?
YUP!

THEN YOU'RE BACK... FOR GOOD?
YUP!

DID YOU MISS ME?
I'M OVER IT.

JENNY, I'M SO HAPPY YOU'RE BACK! THIS IS **AWESOME**!
I **KNOW**!

IT MEANS I GET TO BE WITH **ARTUR** AGAIN!

MMMMMMMM

JENNY, I'M SO HAPPY YOU'RE BACK! THIS IS **AWESOME**!
BEHOLD THE DENIAL.
Peirce

SO LONG, GUYS! I AM TAKE JENNY FOR A "WELCOMING HOME" ICE CREAM!

YOU MUST BE PRETTY PUMPED THAT SHE'S BACK, HUH, ARTUR?
OH, YES, TOTAL PUMP! BUT I **KNOW** SHE WOULD COME BACK!

BECAUSE SHE AND I ARE A **DESTINY** TO BE TOGETHER!

THAT'S SWEET!
REAL SWEET!
SHE SURE IS.
peirce

I DON'T GET IT, NATE. HOW COME YOU'RE SO HAPPY THAT JENNY'S BACK?
WHY WOULDN'T I BE?

BECAUSE A HALF HOUR AGO, YOU WERE MADLY IN LOVE WITH **LILA**!

WHO?

MUST BE NICE TO HAVE A SHORT MEMORY.
EXCEPT IN SOCIAL STUDIES.
Peirce

DAD, ISN'T IT GREAT THAT JENNY'S BACK?
YES, INDEED.
HT

SHE'S SO AWESOME.
I... ER... THOUGHT YOU WERE SWEET ON **LILA**.
ASS'T. COAC

I FOUND OUT THAT LILA HAS A BOYFRIEND.
DOESN'T JENNY HAVE A BOYFRIEND, TOO?

FOR NOW.
I SEE.
Peirce

THAT WAS LILA'S FATHER. SHE'S LEAVING THE TEAM.
AFTER **ONE GAME?**

A COACH FROM A TRAVEL TEAM SAW US PLAY AND RE-CRUITED HER TO PITCH FOR THEM.

WHAT? THERE WAS A **SCOUT** AT OUR GAME? WHY WASN'T **I** SCOUTED, TOO?

YOU WERE KNOCKED UNCONSCIOUS BY A ROUTINE FLY BALL.
OH, RIGHT. NEVER MIND.
Peirce

HEY, DWEEBS! WHAT'S NEW IN DORKVILLE?
GO PLAY IN TRAFFIC, RANDY.

LOOKING FOR SOMEONE TO SIGN YOUR YEARBOOK, WIMPUS?
IT'S...

DON'T MIND IF I DO! THANKS FOR ASKING!
BUT...
NAB!

HMMM, NOW WHAT SHOULD I WRITE? I'LL JUST KEEP IT SIMPLE!

Dear Loser!! How does it feel to be ugly AND stupid?
Smell you later!
Randy

HANG ON TO THIS YEARBOOK! IT'S A COLLECTOR'S ITEM!
OH, IT'S NOT MINE. IT'S MRS. GODFREY'S.

SHE ASKED FRANCIS TO TAKE IT AROUND AND GET KIDS TO SIGN IT!

I CAN'T WAIT TO SHOW IT TO HER!
HAVE A GREAT SUMMER!

NOW THAT JENNY'S BACK, SHE AND ARTUR ARE MORE TOGETHER THAN EVER.
YEAH.

THAT DOESN'T BUM YOU OUT?
FRANCIS, I ACCEPT THAT JENNY DOESN'T LIKE ME THE SAME WAY I LIKE HER... BUT THAT COULD CHANGE SOMEDAY!

I CAN BE PATIENT, MY FRIEND. I CAN BE VERY, VERRRRY PATIENT.

ARE THEY STILL HOLDING HANDS?
NO. NOW THEY'RE KISSING.
Peirce

HOW COME YOU'VE ALWAYS BEEN SO CRAZY ABOUT JENNY?
I JUST **LIKE** HER, THAT'S ALL!
Make
DIFF

BUT YOU'VE LIKED **OTHER** GIRLS BEFORE! YOU WENT OUT WITH ANGIE AND KELLY... YOU HAD A CRUSH ON LILA...

BUT JENNY'S DIFFERENT. SHE HATES ME.

YOU'RE AN UNUSUAL PERSON.
I LIKE A CHALLENGE.
Peirce

Y'KNOW, FRANCIS, YOU HAVE A POINT! EVEN THOUGH JENNY'S MY FIRST CHOICE, THERE ARE LOTS OF **OTHER** GIRLS I LIKE, **TOO**!

WHILE I'M WAITING FOR JENNY TO DUMP ARTUR, WHY SHOULD I SIT AROUND DOING **NOTHING**?

UNTIL SHE AND I GET TOGETHER, I CAN PLAY THE FIELD!

HOW DOES THE FIELD FEEL ABOUT THIS?
HI, LADIES.
Peirce

I JUST GOT BECKY MULLANEY TO SIGN MY YEARBOOK!

NOT TOO **SHABBY**, GETTING THE SCHOOL'S NUMBER ONE **HOTTIE** TO GIVE ME HER SIGNATURE!
SHE SIGNED MINE, TOO!

ACTUALLY, SHE DIDN'T JUST SIGN IT! SHE CALLED ME ADORABLE, GAVE ME HER CELL PHONE NUMBER, AND THEN WROTE "XOXOXO"!

WAIT, SHE TOLD ME SHE DIDN'T HAVE **TIME** TO GIVE ME A PERSONAL MESSAGE!
YEAH, 'CAUSE SHE SPENT SO MUCH TIME ON **CHAD'S**!
WOWZA!
! !

LOOK AT HOW MANY GIRLS SIGNED CHAD'S YEARBOOK!
"CHAD, YOU'RE A SWEETIE"... "CHAD, YOU'RE ADORABLE"...

HOLY COW, CHAD! HOW DO YOU DO IT?
I JUST GO UP TO A GIRL AND SAY...

WILL YOU SIGN MY YEARBOOK?

THAT'S SOME LETHAL CUTENESS RIGHT THERE.
EVEN I WANT TO HUG YOU!
HA HA! YIKES!
Peirce

HI, SHARON!
OH, HI, CHAD!

WILL YOU SIGN MY YEARBOOK?
OF COURSE!

AND WHILE YOU'RE AT IT, WILL YOU SIGN **MINE**, TOO?

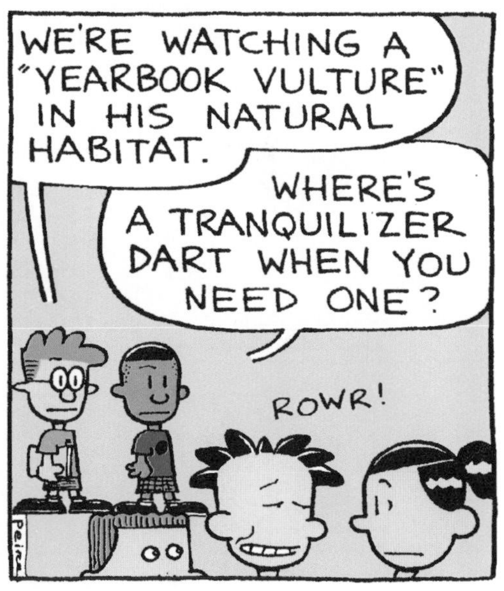
WE'RE WATCHING A "YEARBOOK VULTURE" IN HIS NATURAL HABITAT.
WHERE'S A TRANQUILIZER DART WHEN YOU NEED ONE?
ROWR!
Peirce

"LOCKER SALE"?
YUP!
END-OF-THE-YEAR LOCKER SALE

AS LONG AS I'M CLEANING OUT MY LOCKER ANYWAY, WHY NOT MAKE A PROFIT?

NATE, IS THIS ANOTHER ONE OF YOUR ABSURD "PRANK DAY" TRICKS?
WHAT? TRICKS? NO!

THERE'S ALL KINDS OF QUALITY MERCHANDISE IN HERE!

WE'LL SEE ABOUT THAT!
KLIK!

FOOOMM!
YAAAAAAAAAAAAAAAAHHH...

CLAP CLAP CLAP CLAP
CLAP CLAP CLAP CLAP CLAP
PAY UP.
WORTH EVERY PENNY!
CLAP CLAP CLAP
PRINCIPALOOZA $2
Peirce

HI, TEDDY? WHAT'S THE MATH HOMEWORK FOR TOMORROW?

OH, WAIT A MINUTE! THERE ISN'T ANY HOMEWORK! IT'S SUMMER VACATION!

WA HA HA HA HA
HA HA HA HA HA
HA HA HA HA HA
HA HA HA HA HA

IT TAKES SO LITTLE TO MAKE HIM HAPPY.
NOW YOU CALL ME AND ASK ABOUT THE SCIENCE HOMEWORK!
Peirce

WHAT ARE YOU DOING UP? IT'S THE FIRST DAY OF VACATION! I THOUGHT YOU'D BE SLEEPING IN!
I TRIED.

BUT MY BODY CLOCK IS STILL ON SCHOOL TIME! I WOKE UP AT 6:45! I COULDN'T SLEEP IN!

WELL, AS LONG AS YOU'RE UP, YOU MIGHT AS WELL DO SOMETHING!
I WAS JUST THINKING THAT.

I'LL HAVE A SHORT STACK OF PANCAKES, BACON, AND A SLICE OF MELON.
GOOD. BETTER GET BUSY.
PEIRCE

ARRRGH! IT HAPPENED AGAIN!
6:45

I WOKE UP AT 6:45, AND I DON'T EVEN HAVE TO! SCHOOL'S OVER!

IT HAPPENED AGAIN!

IT HAPPENED AGAIN!!
HOW AWFUL FOR YOU.
Peirce

FOR THE THIRD MORNING IN A ROW, I WOKE UP AT 6:45, EVEN THOUGH I **COULD** HAVE SLEPT 'TIL NOON!

I LAY IN BED **TRYING** TO GO BACK TO SLEEP, BUT IT WAS **HOPELESS**!

FINALLY, I GAVE UP AND CAME HERE.

HOW THOUGHTFUL OF YOU TO WAIT UNTIL 6:50.
IF I HAVE TO SUFFER, **EVERY-ONE** DOES.
Peirce

BEDTIME.
HA HA! I DON'T THINK SO!

I'M TRYING TO GET MY BODY CLOCK OFF OF ITS SCHOOL SCHEDULE! I WANT TO STOP WAKING UP AT 6:45!

SO I JUST DRANK TWO LITERS OF "MOUNTAIN DEW KICKSTART"! I'LL BE UP FOR HOURS!

WELL, THEN, THANK GOODNESS FOR THE "HERE COMES HONEY BOO BOO" MARATHON.
RIGHT! CARE FOR A CHOCOLATE ESPRESSO BEAN?
Peirce

SUCCESS! I'VE READJUSTED MY BODY CLOCK! I'M NO LONGER ON "SCHOOL" SETTING!

INSTEAD OF WAKING UP AT 6:45, I WOKE UP AT 9:30!

TIME TO READJUST YOUR READJUSTMENT.
OH, COME ON!

THEY WERE CERTAINLY **GOOD** DAYS FOR JONAS McBRIDE! BUT THE DECADES **SINCE** THEN HAVE NOT BEEN KIND! HE **NEVER** HAD ANOTHER HIT!

AH, THE 4TH OF JULY FAIR!
YUP! THIS IS A BIG DAY FOR CHAD!

FOR CHAD? HOW COME?
HE'S NEVER BEEN ABLE TO GO ON ANY OF THE RIDES! HE GETS VIOLENTLY ILL!

SO TODAY, I AM GOING TO CURE CHAD OF HIS CHRONIC MOTION SICKNESS!

AND WHAT COULD POSSIBLY GO WRONG?
NO OFFENSE, CHAD, BUT I'M NOT SITTING NEXT TO YOU ON THE "ZIPPER."
OOLP!

HOW LONG HAVE YOU SUFFERED FROM MOTION SICKNESS, CHAD?
MY WHOLE LIFE.

I DO OKAY WHEN I'M GOING STRAIGHT AHEAD. I GET A LITTLE WOOZY WHEN I START GOING BACKWARDS...

...AND SIDEWAYS, AND AROUND AND AROUND, AND... UH... UPSIDE DOWN... AND... UH...
Peirce

I THINK I NEED TO SIT DOWN.
THIS ISN'T STARTING WELL.

HOW ARE YOU GOING TO HELP ME GET OVER MY MOTION SICKNESS?
BY STARTING SLOWLY, CHAD!

YOU'VE GOT TO CRAWL BEFORE YOU CAN WALK! YOU CAN'T JUST CLIMB IN THE "DEATH SPIRAL" AND SAY **GO!**

YOU'VE GOT TO START ON A RIDE THAT'S NOT TOO FAST! NOT TOO SPINNY! A RIDE FOR **BEGINNERS!**

ALL ABOARD THE "CHOO-CHOO CHIPMUNK!"
BUCKLE UP, MISTER! IT'S **TERRIFYING!**

KIDS, YOU'RE TOO OLD TO RIDE THE "LI'L DRAGON!" IT'S FOR THE REAL YOUNG 'UNS!
BUT THIS IS **IMPORTANT**!!

WE'RE TRYING TO CURE CHAD'S MOTION SICKNESS, SO WE'RE STARTING HIM OUT ON SOME KIDDIE RIDES!
NO CAN DO. BOSS'S ORDERS.

I'D BE... AHEM! ...WILLING TO MAKE IT WORTH YOUR WHILE, IF YOU KNOW WHAT I MEAN!

ARE YOU TRYING TO BRIBE ME WITH A TROLL DOLL YOU WON AT THE RING TOSS?
WAIT! I'LL THROW IN A PAIR OF WAX LIPS!

OKAY, CHAD, YOU'VE MADE IT THROUGH ALL THE KIDDIE RIDES WITHOUT GETTING SICK! IT'S TIME TO MOVE UP TO THE MAIN EVENT!
THE "WIDOW MAKER"?

I... I DON'T THINK I'M READY FOR THIS.
SURE YOU ARE! IT'S ALL ABOUT HAVING THE RIGHT MINDSET!

WELL... OKAY. HOLD ON.

READY.
CHAD. CHAD. CHAD.
Peirce

CHAD, YOU DID IT!
OHHHHH...

YOU RODE THE "TWIRLING TEACUPS" WITHOUT GETTING SICK! HOW DO YOU FEEL?
UM... OKAY.

WELL, I THINK YOU'RE MORE THAN OKAY! I'D SAY CONGRATULATIONS ARE IN ORDER!

HOW 'BOUT A NICE BIG PIECE OF FRIED DOUGH?
HLLLP!
peirce

THANKS, ELLEN! I'LL PICK HER UP AT 5:00!
SEE YOU THEN!
BYE, MOM!

WELL, MIRANDA, WHAT SHALL WE DO?
I DON'T KNOW.

WE CAN READ, WE CAN DRAW, WE CAN FILL UP THE WADING POOL...
HMM.

CAN WE PLAY BEAUTY SHOP AND PUT MAKEUP ON SOME DOLLS?
WELL...

I'VE GOT PLENTY OF MAKEUP, BUT I DON'T HAVE DOLLS ANYMORE.
RATS! THEN WHAT'LL WE...

ELLEN, IS NATE AROUND?
HE'S OVER...

...THERE.
Z

KLIK! KLIK! KLIK KLIK! KLIK! KLIK!
THIS IS FUN!
I WILL DESTROY YOU ALL.
KLIK! KLIK!
Peirce

LOOK WHO'S STAYING WITH US FOR A FEW DAYS!
GRAMPS!

BUT WHERE'S GRAM?
SHE'S ON A BUS TRIP WITH THE SENIOR CITIZENS CLUB.

WHY DIDN'T **YOU** GO?
OH, BUS TRIPS AREN'T MY CUP OF TEA.

PLUS, THE SENIOR CITIZENS CLUB HAS BANNED YOU FROM BUS TRIPS FOR LIFE!
NOT FOR LIFE. JUST UNTIL MY 100TH BIRTHDAY.
PEIRCE

DID YOU **REALLY** GET BANNED FROM THE SENIOR CITIZENS BUS TRIP?
YUP.

WHY? GRAMPS, WHAT DID YOU DO?
NOTHING!! I'VE BEEN ON PLENTY OF THEIR BUS TRIPS, AND NOTHING'S HAPPENED!

DAD.

WELL, THERE MAY HAVE BEEN AN UNFORTUNATE INCIDENT IN AMISH COUNTRY.
UNFORTUNATE FOR THE BUGGY DRIVER.
Peirce

SORRY YOU COULDN'T GO ON THE BUS TRIP WITH GRAM, GRAMPS.
DON'T BE SORRY FOR ME, ELLEN.

IT'S NO FUN TO BE COOPED UP ON A BUS OR STUCK IN SOME MUSEUM LOOKING AT ANTIQUE POTTERY!

THAT'S NOT LIVING! I WANT TO LIVE!

WHEEL!... OF!... FORTUNE!
NOW WE'RE COOKIN'!
Peirce

SO, GRAMPS... IS IT TOUGH BEING APART FROM GRAM FOR A FEW DAYS?
NOT AT ALL!

WE'RE NOT A COUPLE OF **NEWLYWEDS**, YOU KNOW! WE'VE BEEN APART BEFORE! I'M A BIG BOY! I CAN HANDLE IT!

HERE YOU GO, GANG! DINNER IS SERVED!

WELCOME TO MY NIGHT-MARE.
LORDY, I MISS THAT WOMAN.

NATE! WHY ON EARTH ARE **YOU** AWAKE?
I COULDN'T SLEEP. I THOUGHT I'D HAVE SOME ICE CREAM.

HA! WELL, GET IN LINE, PAL, BECAUSE THAT'S EXACTLY WHY **I'M**...

HM. THAT'S ODD.

THERE WAS A HALF GALLON OF CHOCO–
SLURP! YOU SNOOZE, YOU LOSE.
HEY!
CHOCO CHUNK

LET 'ER RIP!

WHOA! THAT BALL MOVED!
SMAK!

OOOOOZE...

NATE, HAS GRAMPS BEEN "COACHING" YOU AGAIN?
I SAID JUST A DAB, SON, NOT THE WHOLE TUBE!
PEIRCE

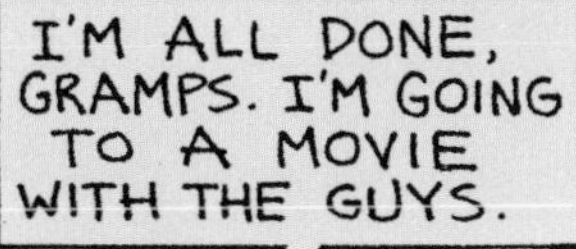
I'M ALL DONE, GRAMPS. I'M GOING TO A MOVIE WITH THE GUYS.

BUT I'M JUST GETTING WARMED UP!
I'LL TAKE OVER, DAD!

HUH?
FATHERS AND SONS! PLAYIN' CATCH!

WE HAVEN'T DONE THIS IN THIRTY YEARS!

IT'LL BE JUST LIKE OLD TIMES!

ZING!

THUD!
OW!

A LITTLE TOO MUCH LIKE OLD TIMES.
I'M TERRIBLY SORRY, MRS. DALRYMPLE.

THIS SHOULD BE FUN! I LOVE BASEBALL!
IF WE WIN, WE'LL BE IN SECOND PLACE!

I HAVEN'T BEEN TO A LITTLE LEAGUE GAME SINCE **YOU** PLAYED, MARTY!
OOH! SPILL IT, GRAMPS!
ASS'T COACH

WAS DAD A DECENT PLAYER AS A KID?
GOOD GRAVY, NO.

BUT HE **TRIED**! HE TRIED!
YEAH, THAT'S HOW HE COACHES, TOO!
PAT PAT
peirce

WHAT'S THE HOLDUP? WHY HASN'T THE GAME STARTED?
THE UMPIRE DIDN'T SHOW UP. WE NEED A FILL-IN.

I'LL FILL IN! LET ME UMP THE GAME!
NO, THAT'S OKAY, DAD. WE'RE LOOKING FOR SOMEONE A BIT... UH... YOUNGER.

WHAT? I'M PLENTY YOUNG, MISTER! I'M IN PERFECT HEALTH! MY MIND IS SHARP AS... AS... UH...

WHAT ARE THOSE POINTY THINGS CALLED?
SIT DOWN, DAD.
Peirce

GREETINGS, GOOD SIR! MAY I JOIN YOU UP HERE IN THE COZY CONFINES OF THE NOSEBLEED SECTION? *CHUCKLE!*

YOU'VE NOTICED MY **CAMERA**, NO DOUBT! YES, YOU'VE GUESSED IT: I'M A PHOTOGRAPHER, DISPATCHED TO SNAP ACTION SHOTS FOR THE LOCAL NEWSPAPER!

UNFORTUNATELY, I KNOW NOTHING ABOUT THE GAME, SO I'LL BE DEPENDING ON **YOU** TO PROVIDE ME WITH EXPLANATIONS DURING KEY MOMENTS!

NOW... WHY IS THAT YOUNGSTER WAVING A STICK AROUND?
HOO BOY.

MY GRANDFATHER'S UP THERE IN THE STANDS! HE'S NEVER SEEN ME PLAY BEFORE!

THIS ONE'S FOR YOU, GRAMPS!

DOOOF!

A NICE GESTURE, BUT A BIT OF AN ANTI-CLIMAX.
NOBODY'S EVER DEDICATED A BRUISE TO ME BEFORE.
Peirce

...AND AFTER ALL THAT, IT TURNED OUT HE WAS TALKING ABOUT THE **ORIGINAL** "BATTLESTAR GALACTICA," NOT THE **RE-BOOT**! HA HA!

...WHICH REMINDS ME OF ANOTHER STORY...
Y'KNOW, I THINK I'M GOING TO CHANGE SEATS.

THIS IS PRIME FOUL BALL TERRITORY. NO SENSE TAKING A LINE DRIVE IN THE OL' COCONUT.

ZOUNDS! THEN **I** SHOULD MOVE, **TOO**!
NO. YOU STAY HERE.
Pairce

IMPRESSIVE GAME, GRANDSON!
WOOOH! WE **SMOKED** THOSE GUYS!

THERE'S NOTHING I ENJOY MORE THAN WATCHING KIDS PLAY BASEBALL!
YEAH, I **LOVE** BASE-BALL!

THE ONLY THING I DON'T LIKE ABOUT IT IS WHEN CRAZY PARENTS SCREAM AT THE COACHES.

I WASN'T SCREAMING, I WAS ENCOURAGING YOU TO RE-ORIENT YOURSELF IN ORDER TO BECOME MORE AWARE OF YOUR SURROUNDINGS.
UH-HUH.

OW. I HAVE A GAS BUBBLE.

MAYBE IT'LL HELP IF I LOOSEN MY BELT.

CRACK!

NAB!

WHUMP!

!

CLICK!
SM

NEXT DAY
"LITTLE LEAGUER CATCHES BALL, DROPS PANTS"!
A "BRIEF" ENCOUNTER WITH FAME!

GRAM!
I'M BACK FROM MY TRIP, AND I'M HERE TO CLAIM MY HUSBAND!

HE HASN'T BEEN DRIVING YOU TOO CRAZY, HAS HE?

NO!
NO!
NYUH.

"NYUH"?
DID I SAY THAT?
THANKS, SON.
Peirce

SO HOW WAS THE SENIOR CITIZENS BUS TRIP, GRAM?
HEAVENLY, HONEY!

WE SAW HISTORICAL SITES, WENT TO A BOTANICAL GARDEN, VISITED A WONDERFUL AQUARIUM... SO MANY MEMORABLE MOMENTS!

BUT THE BEST PART WAS HOW **RELAXING** IT WAS! IT WAS CALM! IT WAS QUIET! IT WAS COMPLETELY STRESS-FREE!

WHAT ARE YOU IMPLYING, MARGE?
OH, RELAX, VERN. I CAME BACK, DIDN'T I?

SO LONG, MARTY! TIME FOR ME TO GET OUT OF YOUR HAIR!

HAIR! HA HA! GET IT?
I GET IT, DAD.

YOU'RE BALD, **TOO**, IN CASE YOU HADN'T NOTICED.
BUT I'M **SUPPOSED** TO BE BALD! I'M **EIGHTY**!

YOU WERE JUST AS BALD WHEN YOU WERE **MY** AGE!!
CAN'T HEAR YOU! I'M DEAF!
OH, VERN! HONESTLY!

YOU AND GRAMPS DIDN'T SEEM TO BE GETTING ALONG SO GREAT WHILE HE WAS HERE.
YOU'RE RIGHT.

PARENTS CAN BE REAL KNUCKLEHEADS SOMETIMES.

SNORT. **TELL** ME ABOUT IT.

WHOOPS.
Peirce

I WISH MY GRANDPARENTS LIVED CLOSER.
YEAH. YOUR GRANDPARENTS ARE AWESOME.

I REMEMBER WHEN YOUR GRANDMOTHER CAME AND STAYED WITH YOU WHEN YOUR DAD THREW HIS BACK OUT.
OHHH, YEAH!

SHE SMELLED LIKE VANILLA AND NUTMEG AND CINNAMON AND... AND...

I'M HUNGRY.
MY GRANDMOTHER SMELLS LIKE MOTHBALLS AND "ICY HOT."
Peirce

I WONDER IF DOGS REMEMBER THEIR GRAND-PARENTS.
I DOUBT THEY EVEN REMEMBER THEIR **PARENTS**.

SPITSY PROBABLY GOT TAKEN AWAY FROM HIS MOTHER WHEN HE WAS... WHAT, EIGHT WEEKS OLD?

SNIFF!

OWOO
OOOO
NICE MOVE.
peirce

ARRGH! INTO THE WATER AGAIN!

WHY DO I PLAY THIS STUPID GAME? WHY?

THAT WAS YOUR LAST BALL.
GOOD! GOOD! BECAUSE I AM DONE!

BUT WE'RE ONLY ON THE FIFTEENTH HOLE!
THAT'S FIFTEEN TOO MANY WHEN YOU STINK LIKE I DO!

LEAVE THE CLUBS! LET SOMEONE ELSE HAVE THEM! I'M NEVER PLAYING ANOTHER ROUND OF GOLF AS LONG AS I...

DAD.

FOUND ANOTHER BALL.

A GOOD CADDY ALWAYS HAS A SPARE.
I THINK I KNOW WHAT I WAS DOING WRONG!
PEIRCE

DAD, I WANT TO GO TO THE MOVIES WITH THE GUYS ON FRIDAY, BUT I DON'T HAVE ANY MONEY.

SO... *AHEM!*... YOU CAN GUESS WHERE I'M GOING WITH THIS.

NOT TO THE MOVIES, OBVIOUSLY.

MAY ALL HIS POPCORN BE STALE.
Peirce

IF YOU NEED MONEY FOR A MOVIE, NATE, GO OUT AND **EARN** IT!

FIND A JOB THAT NEEDS DOING, AND THEN **DO** IT!

OKAY?
OKAY.

HOW MUCH WILL YOU PAY ME TO TRIM YOUR NOSE HAIR?
I DO MY OWN MAN-SCAPING.

MR. EUSTIS, GOT ANY ODD JOBS THAT NEED DOING?
AS A MATTER OF FACT, I DO.
STATE

LAST FALL, I PAID YOU TWENTY DOLLARS TO MOVE THOSE ROCKS OVER THERE...AND YOU ONLY GOT HALF-WAY THROUGH!
STATE

FINISH THAT JOB, AND THEN MAYBE... MAYBE... I'LL FIND SOMETHING ELSE FOR YOU TO DO!
STATE

EPIC FAIL ON THE "KINDLY NEXT-DOOR NEIGHBOR" STRATEGY.
REMEMBER, LIFT WITH YOUR LEGS.
Peirce

A **LEMONADE STAND?** HOW LAME CAN YOU GET?
JUST TRYIN' TO MAKE A LITTLE MONEY, GINA.
LEMONADE
50¢

SNORT! YEAH, **VERY** LITTLE!
AS USUAL, YOU HAVE NO IDEA WHAT YOU'RE TALKING ABOUT.
LEMONADE

...BUT HERE. JUST BECAUSE I'M SUCH A NICE GUY, I'LL LET YOU TRY A FREE SAMPLE!
LEMONADE
50¢

HNNGK!
OF COURSE, IF YOU WANT ME TO ADD SUGAR, YOU'LL HAVE TO PAY FULL FREIGHT.
LEMONADE

HI, LADY, DO YOU HAVE ANY WORK I COULD DO TO EARN SOME MONEY?

COME TO THINK OF IT, I **DO** HAVE AN ODD JOB!

YOU CAN SCRUB ALL THE BIRD DROPPINGS OFF MY LAWN ORNAMENTS!

TWO HOURS AT THE CINEPLEX ISN'T WORTH THIS.
THIS ONE'S NAMED "PEEPERS"!
SHK
SHK
SHK
SHK
PEIRCE

THIS MOVIE BETTER BE GOOD. I BUSTED MY BUTT ALL WEEK TO SAVE UP FOR THIS.
ARRGH! "WOLVERINE" IS **SOLD OUT**!
NOW

WHAT?
HOW 'BOUT WE SEE "THE CONJURING?"
DUDE, THAT'S RATED **R**!

WELL, I'M **NOT** WATCHING SOME CHICK FLICK!
THAT LEAVES US WITH ONLY ONE CHOICE.
Peirce

THIS IS AN OUTRAGE.
HEY, EVERYONE! I HAVE A **SMURF-TASTIC** IDEA!

IF YOU COULD ONLY LISTEN TO ONE SONG FOR THE REST OF YOUR LIFE, WHAT WOULD IT BE?
WHY WOULD THAT HAPPEN?

IT'S A **HYPOTHETICAL**, FRANCIS! IF YOU HAD A RADIO THAT COULD ONLY PLAY **ONE SONG**...

...WHAT SONG WOULD YOU PICK?
I WOULDN'T **HAVE** TO PICK! I COULD LISTEN TO SONGS ON **OTHER** PEOPLE'S RADIOS!

WHAT IF THERE **WERE** NO OTHER RADIOS?
I'D **SING** WHATEVER SONGS I WANTED TO HEAR!

LET'S SAY YOU WERE **MUTE**, THEN!
SO WHAT? I COULD STILL PLAY ANY SONG ON A GUITAR OR A PIANO OR A...

OKAY, **OKAY**! THEN WHAT IF YOU WERE **DEAF**?

IF YOU WERE DEAF, AND YOU COULD ONLY LISTEN TO ONE... UH... ONE...

YOU RUIN EVERYTHING.
♫

MY MOM MADE BROWNIES!
OOH! DON'T MIND IF I DO!

BROWNIE, CHAD?
I'M NOT ALLOWED. MY GRAM PUT ME ON A DIET.

BUT... THEY SMELL SO GOOD... I DON'T KNOW IF... I'M NOT SURE I... I...

SECONDS LATER...
CHAD'S A LITTLE SCARY WHEN HIS SURVIVAL INSTINCTS KICK IN.
NARF NARF NARF NARF NARF

HOW COME YOUR GRANDMOTHER PUT YOU ON A DIET, CHAD?
SHE THINKS I'M FAT.

OF COURSE, SHE NEVER COMES OUT AND **SAYS** THAT! SHE JUST FINDS WAYS TO **REMIND** ME OF IT!

"HERE, HONEY, WHY DON'T YOU TRY A **CARROT STICK**!"
"REMEMBER, YOUR STOMACH IS **FULL** TWENTY MINUTES BEFORE YOU **REALIZE** IT!"

"WHAT'S ON TV? OH, **LOOK**! IT'S '**THE BIGGEST LOSER**'!"
POOR CHAD.
Peirce

DON'T LISTEN TO YOUR GRANDMOTHER, CHAD! YOU'RE NOT FAT! YOU JUST HAVEN'T HAD A GROWTH SPURT YET!

ONCE YOU HIT PUBERTY, YOU'LL STRETCH OUT!
REALLY? YOU THINK I COULD BE LEAN AND MEAN?

LEAN, YES. MEAN, NO.
BUT WHY NOT?

BECAUSE YOU'RE CHAD.
IT'S THE DIMPLES, DUDE.
Peirce

I WISH MY GRAM WASN'T SO FOCUSED ON HOW MUCH I WEIGH.

SHE ALWAYS SAYS, "IF YOU LIE ABOUT YOUR WEIGHT, THE ONLY PERSON YOU'RE FOOLING IS YOURSELF!"

SO I TOLD HER, "I'LL STOP LYING ABOUT MY WEIGHT IF YOU STOP LYING ABOUT YOUR AGE."

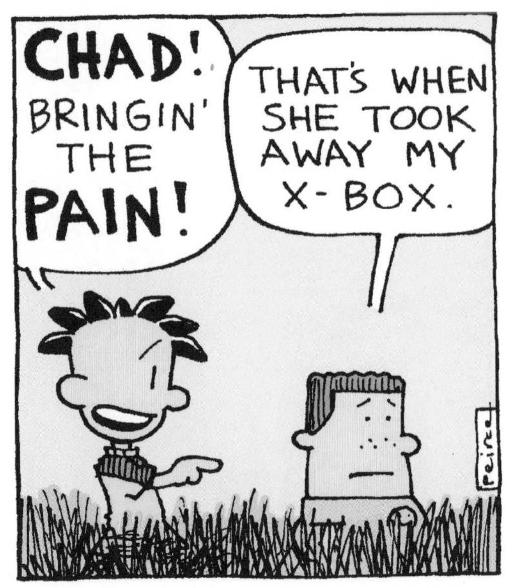
CHAD! BRINGIN' THE PAIN!
THAT'S WHEN SHE TOOK AWAY MY X-BOX.
Peirce

HOW GOES THE DIET, CHAD?
MY GRAM GAVE ME SOME SNAK.

OOH! WHAT KIND OF SNACK?
NOT SNACK. **S.N.A.K.**

SOY NUTS AND KALE.

THAT'S JUST WRONG.
THIS IS AN ALL-TIME LOW IN THE HISTORY OF FOOD ACRONYMS.
Peirce

NOW LISTEN UP, GUYS! IT'S EASIER TO DO JUST ABOUT ANYTHING IN A **GROUP**, RIGHT?

CHAD'S ON A DIET! SO LET'S **ALL** GO ON A DIET! Y'KNOW, FOR SOLIDARITY!

WE'LL EAT THE SAME STUFF **YOU** EAT, CHAD! WE'LL ALL BE IN IT **TOGETHER**!

THAT MEANS YOU'LL HAVE TO GIVE UP CHEEZ DOODLES.
WELL, THAT'S ENOUGH TOGETHERNESS FOR ONE DAY...
SHOVE!
Peirce

OH, COME **ON**!
DAD? CAN I HIT ONE?

NATE, CADDIES AREN'T SUPPOSED TO...
BUT THERE'S NOBODY BEHIND US! JUST ONE SHOT?

WELL... OKAY, **ONE**.
YESS!

BUT REMEMBER, YOU'RE A **BEGINNER**.

YOU CAN'T EXPECT TO MAKE SOLID CONTACT ON YOUR FIRST TRY!

GOLF ISN'T AN EASY GAME, YOU KNOW! IN FACT, IT'S PROBABLY THE MOST DIFFICULT GAME IN THE **WORLD**!

IT'S EXACTING! IT'S BAFFLING!

POW!

IT'S COMPLETELY, UTTERLY HUMILIATING.
I'M ON THE GREEN!
Peirce

WHAT'S UP?
JUST RE-ORGANIZING MY ROOM, FRANCIS!
BRUI

EVERY SO OFTEN, I GET THE URGE TO LIBERATE MYSELF FROM SOME OF THE STUFF THAT PILES UP!

LIKE THIS, YOU MEAN?
WHAT IS IT?

MY iPOD!
OH. YOU CAN HAVE THAT.
Peirce

THERE! I'VE RE-DONE MY BULLETIN BOARD TO DISPLAY ALL MY ART MASTERPIECES!

THEY... UH... ALL KIND OF LOOK ALIKE.
NO **DUH**, FRANCIS! I'M EXPLORING A **THEME**!

PICASSO HAD HIS "BLUE" PERIOD... GAUGUIN HAD HIS "TROPICAL" PERIOD...

I HAVE MY "MRS. GODFREY BEING ATTACKED BY WILD ANIMALS" PERIOD.
I'VE NEVER SEEN CHIPMUNKS LOOK QUITE SO VICIOUS.
Peirce

...AND OVER HERE IS MY TROPHY SHELF!

AH! MY MVP AWARD FROM OUR THIRD GRADE BASKETBALL TEAM!
UH... YOU WEREN'T THE MVP.

SURE I WAS! COACH KEVIN SAID I WAS THE GLUE THAT HELD THE TEAM TOGETHER!
HE TOLD ALL OF US THAT.

THAT I WAS THE GLUE THAT HELD US TOGETHER?
WE HAVE A LOT OF CONVER-SATIONS LIKE THIS.
Peirce

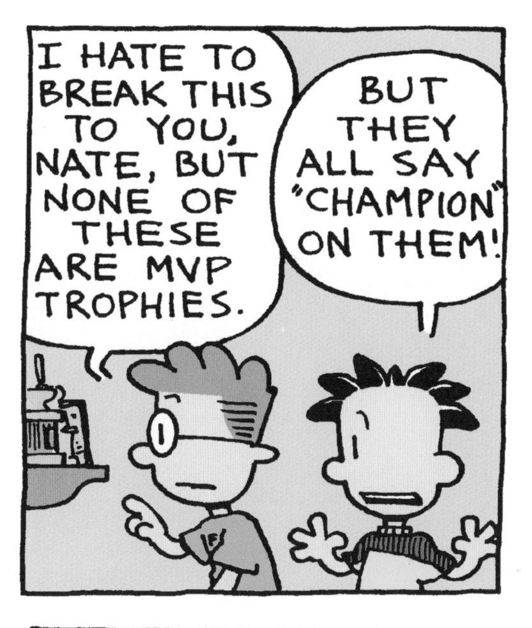
I HATE TO BREAK THIS TO YOU, NATE, BUT NONE OF THESE ARE MVP TROPHIES.
BUT THEY ALL SAY "CHAMPION" ON THEM!

WE **ALL** GOT TROPHIES THAT SAID "CHAMPION"! THAT'S THE WAY THEY DO IT WITH REALLY LITTLE KIDS!

WHO GAVE YOU THE IDEA THAT YOU WERE THE MVP?

SO!
NOW WHAT DID I DO?
Peirce

HOW COME YOU TOLD ME I WAS THE MVP OF MY THIRD GRADE BASKETBALL TEAM?
WHAT? I DIDN'T!

I SAID YOU WERE AN IMPORTANT PART OF THE TEAM! **YOU** SOMEHOW TURNED THAT INTO WINNING THE MVP AWARD!

YOU HEARD WHAT YOU WANTED TO HEAR.

IT'S ALL IN MY MIND.
AT LEAST **SOME-** THING'S IN THERE!

OKAY, SO MAYBE I DIDN'T WIN THE MVP AWARD ON OUR THIRD GRADE TEAM. NOT OFFICIALLY.

BUT COACH KEVIN THOUGHT I WAS THE MVP! I KNOW HE DID! AND COACH KEVIN HAD GREAT JUDGMENT!

WOULD THAT BE THE SAME COACH KEVIN WHO'S CURRENTLY IN PRISON FOR CHECK FORGERY?

AT LEAST THAT'S WHAT HIS FOURTH WIFE TOLD MY MOM!
SHUT UP.
PEIRCE

WE'RE OUT OF SUNSCREEN. I'M GONNA GET SOME MORE AT THE SNACK BAR.
NO, DON'T!

THE SNACK BAR'S A TOTAL RIP-OFF! THEY CHARGE TEN BUCKS FOR ONE LITTLE TUBE!

SO WHAT AM I SUPPOSED TO DO, BURN TO A CRISP?
NO, JUST USE A CHEAPER ALTER-NATIVE!

YOGURT?
WHY NOT? IT COVERS UP JUST AS WELL AS SUNSCREEN!
GLOP!

WANT SOME? THERE'S PLENTY LEFT!

SKWAK!
HEY!

GAH!

GET OFF ME, YOU DISGUSTING SKY RATS!
THERE'S PLENTY LEFT!
I'LL GET A SPOON!

HAVE YOU NOTICED NATE SEEMS KIND OF... PREOCCUPIED LATELY?
YEAH. I GUESS.

I WONDER WHAT'S BOTHERING HIM. I WONDER IF IT'S SERIOUS.
I DOUBT IT. IT'S PROBABLY SOMETHING STUPID.

I'M BETTING SERIOUS.
I'M BETTING STUPID.

GUYS, I THINK I'VE BEEN ABDUCTED BY ALIENS.
YOU WIN.

YOU THINK YOU'VE BEEN ABDUCTED BY ALIENS?
YUP.

THEY'VE BEEN TAKING ME ABOARD THEIR SPACESHIP EVERY NIGHT WHILE I SLEEP.

AND WHY'S THAT?
HOW SHOULD I KNOW, FRANCIS? THEY HAVEN'T TOLD ME THEIR MASTER PLAN!

ALL I KNOW IS, THEY'VE BEEN SCANNING MY BRAIN.
ARE YOU SURE THEY DIDN'T REMOVE IT ALTOGETHER?

I'VE BEEN READING UP ON IT, AND I'VE GOT ALL THE CHARACTERISTICS OF AN ALIEN ABDUCTEE!

LIKE A VIVID IMAGINATION?
NO, LIKE **LOST TIME!**

THERE ARE HOURS AND HOURS THAT GO BY, AND I CAN'T REMEMBER **ANYTHING!**
YEAH, THAT'S HAPPENED TO ME, TOO.

IT'S CALLED "SCHOOL!"
NEXT TIME, ASK THEM TO ABDUCT MRS. GODFREY!
Peirce

IF YOU'VE REALLY BEEN ABDUCTED BY ALIENS, TELL ME WHAT THEY LOOK LIKE.
I DON'T **KNOW**!

THEY ERASE MY MEMORY BEFORE THEY RETURN ME TO EARTH! SO I CAN'T PICTURE THEIR FACES!

BUT I DO HAVE A FAINT MEMORY OF A MILKY WAY.

THE GALAXY?
THE CANDY BAR. I WAS HUNGRY WHEN I WOKE UP.
Peirce

IF YOU WANT US TO BELIEVE YOU'RE AN ALIEN ABDUCTEE, NATE, YOU'LL HAVE TO SHOW US SOME **PROOF**!

I DON'T **HAVE** ANY PROOF!
THEN HOW DO YOU KNOW IT HAPPENED?

I JUST **DO**! I CAN'T EXPLAIN WHY, BUT I **KNOW** I'VE BEEN TAKEN ABOARD AN ALIEN SHIP!

PLUS, YOU'VE BEEN BINGE-WATCHING ALL NINE SEASONS OF "THE X-FILES."
WHAT ARE YOU IMPLYING?
AGENT SCULLY! ROWR!

OF MY **ALIEN ABDUCTION**, FRANCIS! THEY CAME AGAIN LAST NIGHT AND TOOK ME ONTO THEIR SPACESHIP!

REALLY? SHE SAID THAT?
THAT'S WHAT FRANCIS TOLD ME!
HEY!

COACH JOHN!
WHAT'S GOING ON HERE, SCRUBS?

WE'RE... Y'KNOW... JUGGLING.
YEAH. GETTING READY FOR THE SEASON.
OH, REALLY?

EXCUSE ME, BUT SOCCER PLAYERS DON'T TRAIN BY DOING USELESS BALL TRICKS!

THEY TRAIN BY GETTING THEMSELVES IN TIP-TOP CONDITION!!
AND HOW DO THEY DO THAT?

THEY RUN THEIR BUTTS OFF!

SPEAKING OF BUTTS, I'VE GOT A PAIN IN MINE.
THIS IS AN OUTRAGE.
PEIRCE

FRANCIS. YELL AT ME.
SAY **WHAT**?

SCHOOL STARTS NEXT WEEK! MRS. GODFREY WILL BE AIRING ME OUT, ALL DAY **EVERY** DAY!

I CAN'T WALK INTO THAT KIND OF VERBAL ABUSE WITHOUT BEING **READY** FOR IT! I'VE GOT TO GET IN **SHAPE**!

HIS PRE-SEASON CONDITIONING PROGRAM ISN'T LIKE MOST PEOPLE'S.
THAT IS THE STUPIDEST THING I EVER–
LOUDER.
PEIRCE

MY GOAL IS TO GET SO USED TO MRS. GODFREY YELLING AT ME THAT I NO LONGER HEAR IT.

SHOULDN'T YOUR GOAL BE TO ACT IN SUCH A WAY THAT SHE WON'T **HAVE** TO YELL AT YOU?

SORRY.
TEDDY, LET'S START A FRANCIS-SIZED HOLE RIGHT HERE.

IF YOU DON'T WANT TO GET SICK, YOU HAVE TO BUILD UP YOUR RESISTANCE TO GERMS, RIGHT?
I GUESS.

THAT'S WHAT I'M DOING! BUILDING UP MY RESISTANCE TO MRS. GODFREY!
NOW: SAY SOMETHING MEAN.

YOU HAVE STUPID HAIR!
NO, NO, NO! SAY SOMETHING LIKE GODFREY WOULD SAY IT!

YOU'RE THE WARREN HARDING OF SOCIAL STUDIES STUDENTS!
AND YOU HAVE STUPID HAIR!
I HATE YOU GUYS.

HOW AM I SUPPOSED TO GET MYSELF READY FOR ANOTHER YEAR OF MRS. GODFREY WITH YOU CLOWNS FOOLING AROUND?
HEH HEH
OW!

HERE, I'VE WRITTEN OUT SOME GODFREY-ISH DIALOGUE! I'LL BE ME, AND TEDDY, YOU BE MRS. GODFREY!

AHEM! "NATE, YOU HAVE SO MUCH POTENTIAL, IF ONLY YOU'D..."
OH, COME ON. I CAN'T DO THIS.
WHY NOT?

IT'S TOTALLY UNREALISTIC!
CAN I CHANGE IT TO "YOU HAVE **NO** POTENTIAL?"

GO AHEAD AND JOKE ABOUT IT, YOU GUYS, BUT I'VE GOT TO PREPARE MYSELF FOR MRS. GODFREY **SCREAMING** AT ME FOR THE NEXT TEN MONTHS!
SNICKER!

IF YOU'RE NOT GOING TO HELP ME, I'LL GET READY ON MY **OWN**!

OW!
ZING!

WHAT ARE YOU DOING, YOU STUPID KID?
NOW WE'RE COOKIN'!

It's hot and sunny, yes.
But still...

ONLY TWO MORE DAYS OF SUMMER.
DON'T REMIND ME.
I WONDER WHAT SCHOOL WILL BE LIKE THIS YEAR.

PROBABLY THE SAME AS EVER.
I NEED A SIGN.

A SIGN?
YES, A SIGN! SOME KIND OF MESSAGE!

I WANT TO KNOW WHAT'S COMING! I WANT TO KNOW WHAT TO EXPECT!

SO GET YOUR PALM READ.
I DON'T MEAN **THAT** KIND OF SIGN, TEDDY!

I'M TALKING ABOUT THE KIND OF SIGN THAT SHOWS UP WHEN YOU LEAST...

WHAT DO YOU THINK IT MEANS?
NO IDEA!

UGH. SCHOOL STARTS TOMORROW.
ANY NEW SCHOOL YEAR'S RESO-LUTIONS?

SAY WHAT?
WITH YOUR TRACK RECORD, IT MIGHT BE A GOOD IDEA TO PUT YOUR BEST FOOT FORWARD.

YOU KNOW, FRANCIS, YOU'RE RIGHT! I **WILL** PUT MY BEST FOOT FORWARD!

DOOF!

LISTEN TO 'EM ALL.

THEY DON'T HAVE TO GO TO SCHOOL.

CRICKETS ARE LUCKY.

END-OF-SUMMER HAIKU

ARE YOU COMING IN OR NOT?
JUST PREPARING MYSELF.

WHEN YOU ENTER A SCHOOL BUILDING FOR THE FIRST TIME, IT MESSES UP THE PRESSURE IN YOUR HEAD.

OW!
SEE? MY EARS JUST GOT ALL PLUGGED UP!

YOU KNOW WHAT HELPS WITH THAT? CHEWING GUM.
I HATE THIS PLACE.
NO GUM CHEWING
Peirce

WELCOME BACK, BOYS!
MR. NICHOLS, ARE THERE ANY TEACHER CHANGES THIS YEAR?

CHANGES?
ANY RETIREMENTS? ANY FIRINGS? ANY ARRESTS?

NATE, YOU'LL BE DELIGHTED TO KNOW THAT OUR FACULTY IS EXACTLY THE SAME AS IT WAS A YEAR AGO!

WHAT A BUZZKILL.
FOR THERE TO BE A BUZZ-KILL, DOESN'T THERE HAVE TO BE A BUZZ?
Peirce

GOOD MORNING, FRANCIS! GOOD MORNING, TEDDY!

NATE! FOR HEAVEN'S SAKE, STRAIGHTEN UP! YOU'RE SLOUCHING!
ME? SLOUCHING?

GEE, WHY WOULD I BE SLOUCH-ING?

COULD IT BE ALL THE PRESSURE YOU PILE ON ME??
GONNA BE A LONG YEAR.
PEIRCE

MR. ROSA, I'M GOING TO NEED YOUR HELP THIS YEAR.
WELL, NATE, I'LL TRY TO TEACH YOU ALL I KNOW!

NO, NO, I DON'T NEED YOU TO **TEACH** ME! I NEED YOU TO **REPRESENT** ME!

I'M OFFER-ING YOU THE CHANCE TO BE MY AGENT.

IT'S A SIMPLE JOB: SELL MY PAINTINGS ON THE INTERNET AND KEEP ME OUT OF THE TABLOIDS.
HOO BOY.
PEIRCE

PEOPLE, I'VE FORGOTTEN WHERE WE LEFT OFF LAST YEAR.
NATE, WHY DON'T YOU **REMIND** ME?
HUH?
WHAT WERE WE STUDYING WHEN SCHOOL ENDED IN JUNE?

HOW AM **I** SUPPOSED TO REMEMBER WHEN **YOU** DON'T?
I **DO** REMEMBER!

THEN WHY DID YOU SAY YOU DIDN'T?
TO GET YOUR **ATTENTION!** BUT **OBVIOUSLY,** NATE, I REMEMBER!

SO YOU WERE **LYING** WHEN YOU SAID YOU DIDN'T REMEMBER?
OH, FOR HEAVEN'S SAKE.

I MEAN, IF WE CAN'T **TRUST** YOU...
ALL RIGHT, ALL **RIGHT**! WE WERE STUDYING THE COX-BREMERTON TREATY!

THAT'S WHAT **I** WAS GOING TO SAY! THE COX-BREMERTON TREATY!

THERE'S NO SUCH THING AS THE COX-BREMERTON TREATY.
!

PUNK'D!
SHE'S EVIL.

JENNY, M'LADY!
I'M NOT YOUR LADY.

WHERE WERE YOU ALL SUMMER? AFTER YOU MOVED BACK FROM SEATTLE, I NEVER SAW YOU!

THE PEOPLE WHO I WANTED TO SEE ME SAW ME.

YES, I WAS SEE HER ALL SUMMER LONG!
THANKS, ARTUR.
Peirce

CHESTER, MY MAN!

HOW WAS YOUR SUMMER? WHAT DID YOU DO?

MY PARENTS SENT ME TO A CAMP FOR KIDS WHO NEED HELP CONTROLLING THEIR ANGER.

HEEEY, THAT'S GREA-
NOW GO AWAY OR I'LL RIP YOUR ARM OFF.
Peirce

NATE, PLEASE TELL THE CLASS WHY THE WAR OF 1812 WAS FOUGHT.

BECAUSE THE TWO SIDES JUST COULDN'T AGREE! WHY, OH **WHY** CAN'T WE ALL JUST **GET ALONG**?

THAT'S VERY TOUCHING. AND WHO **WERE** THE TWO SIDES?

HISTORIANS ARE STILL DEBATING THAT.
CRIPES.
Peirce

ANSWER THIS QUESTION, NATE: DURING THE WAR OF 1812...
MRS. GODFREY...

I RESPECTFULLY REFUSE TO ANSWER ANY QUESTIONS ABOUT WAR. I'M A PACIFIST.

YOU'RE A PACIFIST.
RIGHT.

THEN WHY DID YOU HIT RANDY IN THE HEAD WITH YOUR SCIENCE TEXTBOOK YESTERDAY?
IT WAS THE ONLY HARDCOVER I HAD.
Peirce

MRS. GODFREY, THERE'S SOMETHING I HAVE TO TELL YOU. I JUST CAN'T HOLD IT IN ANYMORE!

WELL, MY GOODNESS, GINA! WHAT **IS** IT?

NATE'S DRAWING AN INSULTING PICTURE OF YOU **RIGHT NOW**!
!
!
EX

NATE. GET UP HERE!
OH, HOW I HATE THEM.
Peirce

I JUST THOUGHT OF SOMETHING.

IN EVERY SINGLE CLASS, I SIT EITHER IN FRONT OF, BEHIND, OR RIGHT NEXT TO **GINA!**

MUST BE **LOVE!**
HEH HEH!

HA HA HA HA
NOBODY UNDERSTANDS MY SUFFERING.
HA
HA HA
HA
HA HA

WELL, HEY THERE, FELLA! HI!

DID YOU SEE THAT, FRANCIS? THAT DOG CAME RIGHT UP TO ME!
SO?

SO, YOU'D NEVER SEE A CAT DO THAT!

DOGS ARE FRIENDLY! CATS JUST SIT AROUND ALL DAY LICKING THEMSELVES!

EVEN YOU HAVE TO ADMIT THAT DOGS ARE FRIENDLIER THAN CATS!
OKAY, OKAY! DOGS ARE FRIENDLIER THAN CATS!

GRRRRRRRRR
!
!

...WITH A FEW PSYCHOTIC EXCEPTIONS.
WANNA TRADE BRANCHES?
WOOF! WOOF!
WOOF! WOOF! WOOF! WOOF!

PRINCIPAL NICHOLS, CAN WE CHANGE OUR SCHOOL MASCOT?
CHANGE IT? WHY?

WHAT'S WRONG WITH "BOBCATS"?
YOU JUST SAID IT! BOBCATS! BOB**CATS**!

I **HATE** CATS! THEY'RE SO... SO...

...SO **FELINE**!
YES, THAT **IS** ANNOYING.
Peirce

I DON'T THINK OUR MASCOT SHOULD BE A BOBCAT ANYMORE! IT SHOULD BE SOME KIND OF DOG!
WHY A DOG?

BECAUSE DOGS ARE **BETTER** THAN CATS, TEDDY! DOGS ARE SUPERIOR IN EVERY CONCEIVABLE...

WURF?
SPITSY, YOUR TIMING BLOWS.
Peirce

MR. STAPLES, WE'RE LOOKING FOR MASCOT SUGGESTIONS. WHAT WAS **YOUR** MASCOT WHEN **YOU** WERE IN MIDDLE SCHOOL?

WE WERE THE "FIGHTIN' WOMBATS!"

5
7

MATH TEACHERS ARE USELESS IN SO MANY WAYS.
IS A WOMBAT LIKE A ZOMBIE?

HERE'S WHAT I WANT TO KNOW: WHY ARE WE CALLED THE BOBCATS IN THE FIRST PLACE?

MASCOTS ARE SUPPOSED TO BE NATIVE SPECIES! HAVE YOU EVER SEEN A BOBCAT AROUND HERE? I HAVEN'T!

OUR MASCOT SHOULD BE AN ANIMAL THAT LIVES AROUND HERE!

THE OTHER DAY, I SAW A ONE-LEGGED PIGEON!
YOU'RE NOT HELPING, CHAD.

SO YOU THINK WE SHOULD HAVE A MASCOT THAT'S MORE... LOCAL?
RIGHT! LIKE THE FLORIDA GATORS!

WHEN PEOPLE GO TO FLORIDA, THEY SEE GATORS! WHEN THEY COME **HERE**, THEY SEEEE...

MOOSE!
SEAGULLS!
BLACK FLIES!

WE'RE NOT GOING TO BE THE P.S. 38 **BLACK FLIES!**
HOW ABOUT ROADKILL?
peirce

HOW GOES THE QUEST TO CHANGE THE SCHOOL MASCOT?
I'M GIVING UP.

NATE!
WHAT? **WHY**? YOU WERE SO GUNG-HO ABOUT IT!

I HEARD YOU WANT A NEW MASCOT, AND I HAVE A **FABULOUS** SUGGESTION: A **UNICORN**!

LOVE IT, SUZY!
UNICORNS ARE MAGICAL
YAAY!
I'VE SORT OF LOST CONTROL OF THE PROCESS.
OOH!
IDEA!
CLAP
CLAP
CLAP
Peirce

NATE.
GAH!

THAT'S SUPPOSED TO BE A PICTURE OF **ME**, I SUPPOSE?
WHA-? NO! **NO!**

I'LL... KOFF! ... I'LL PUT IT AWAY.
NO, DON'T!

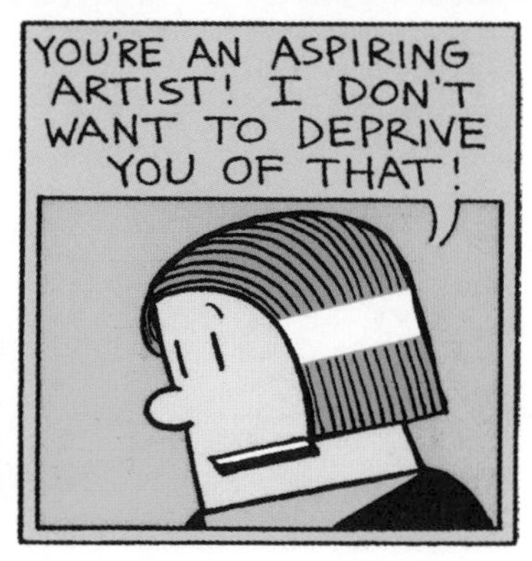
YOU'RE AN ASPIRING ARTIST! I DON'T WANT TO DEPRIVE YOU OF THAT!

WHAT KIND OF TEACHER WOULD I BE IF I DIDN'T HELP YOU DEVELOP YOUR TALENTS?
UH...

THE REST OF YOU ARE DISMISSED EARLY. GO TO THE GYM OR THE LIBRARY.
OOH! YAY!
YES!

NATE AND I WILL STAY HERE AND WORK ON IMPROVING HIS **ART SKILLS!**

DRAW.
CRIPES.

WHAT'S UP, FELLAS?
TEDDY FOUND A NOTE.
PART OF A NOTE.

IT LOOKS LIKE SOME-ONE RIPPED IT UP. THIS PIECE WAS UNDER A TABLE IN THE LIBRARY.
WHAT'S IT SAY?

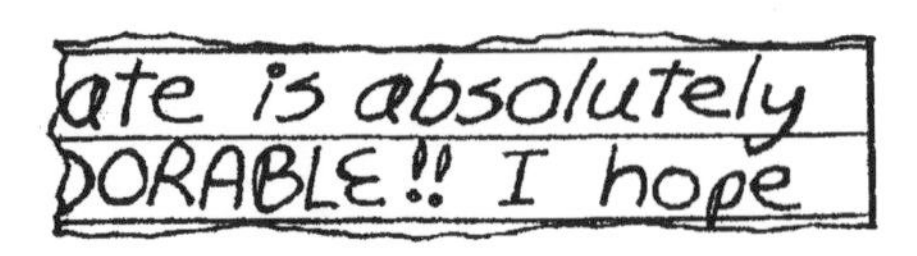
ate is absolutely
DORABLE!! I hope

SOMEBODY THINKS I'M ADORABLE!!
IT'S GOTTA BE A HOAX.

OBVIOUSLY, WHOEVER WROTE THIS NOTE WAS TALKING ABOUT ME!
IT'S A POSSIBILITY.

BUT WHO DID WRITE IT? THAT'S THE MYSTERY! THIS IS A JOB FOR...

ZING!

THE SUSPENSE IS KILLING ME.
GREETINGS, CHAPS.

NATE WRIGHT, PRIVATE EYE, AT YOUR SERVICE.
OH, GOODY.
F

THE TASK AT HAND IS TO THOROUGHLY INVESTIGATE THIS SCRAP OF A **NOTE** THAT TEDDY FOUND!

WHO WROTE IT? **WHERE** IS THE REST OF IT? **WHAT** DOES IT SAY?

WHY ARE YOU TALKING LIKE STEWIE FROM "FAMILY GUY"?
AND **WHEN** WILL IT STOP?
Peirce

ate is absolutely
DORABLE!! I hope
WHOEVER WROTE THIS NOTE WAS WRITING ABOUT ME!
HOW DO YOU KNOW?

DEDUCTIVE REASONING, FRANCIS! WHO ELSE AT P.S. 38 HAS A NAME ENDING IN A-T-E?
TATE GIBSON.

NO. NO, THIS NOTE COULDN'T HAVE BEEN WRITTEN ABOUT TATE GIBSON.
AND WHY NOT?

BECAUSE HE DOESN'T HAVE MY DEVIL-MAY-CARE CHARISMA, OLD BEAN.
I'M SO GLAD YOU'RE APPROACHING THIS SCIENTIFICALLY.
Peirce

ate is absolutely
DORABLE!! I hope
THE QUESTION IS: WHAT MYSTERY GIRL WROTE THIS NOTE?
HOW DO YOU KNOW IT'S A GIRL?

YOU **THINK** THE NOTE'S ABOUT YOU, AND YOU **THINK** A GIRL WROTE IT! BUT WHY ARE YOU SO **SURE**?

BECAUSE BOYS DON'T USE THE WORD "ADORABLE," OLD SPORT.

THEY ALSO DON'T DRESS LIKE SHERLOCK HOLMES AND SMOKE BUBBLE PIPES.
CHUCKLE! TOUCHÉ.
HA! NOW **THAT'S** ADORABLE!
Peirce

MAYBE MY ULTRA-AMAZING SENSE OF SMELL WILL HELP ME FIGURE OUT WHO WROTE THIS NOTE!

LET'S SEE... I SMELL PAPER... INK... UMM... A SLIGHT HINT OF HAND SOAP... A FAINT SCENT OF LAVENDER PERFUME...
SNIFF
SNUFF
SNIFF

AND...AGH! I SMELL SOMETHING **NASTY**! IT'S... *KOFF!*... IT'S LIKE ROTTEN EGGS! OR A **DEAD ANIMAL**!

WELCOME TO OUR WORLD.
OH. WAIT.
Peirce

HI, MR. ROSA!
HELLO, NATE!

ER... WHAT'S NEW?
OH, YOU KNOW... SOLVING MYSTERIES AND STUFF.

I DIDN'T KNOW YOU WERE IN THE BUSINESS OF SOLVING MYSTERIES.
YOU'RE NOT **SUPPOSED** TO KNOW!

WE PRIVATE DETECTIVES LIKE TO KEEP A LOW PROFILE.
HENCE THE HAL-LOWEEN COSTUME AND BUBBLE PIPE.
Peirce

I WAS **TOTALLY** CRACKING UP!
PFFT. I SAW THAT MOVIE, TOO. IT WAS LAME.

...SAID THE GUY WITH NO SENSE OF HUMOR.
WHEN SOME-THING'S FUNNY, I LAUGH.

BET **I** CAN MAKE YOU LAUGH, FRANCIS!
OOH! BET **I** CAN **FIRST**!

WHAT DID ONE SNOWMAN SAY TO THE OTHER? "HEY, DO YOU SMELL CARROTS?"

WHAT'S BROWN AND STICKY?
CHUCKLE! A **STICK**!
YAWNNN

WHY DID THE DUCK... OOF!
OKAY, THAT'S IT! AMATEUR HOUR IS OVER!

OBSERVE THE HILARITY!

YANK!

Peirce

THE SECRET TO SOLVING THIS MYSTERY IS **HANDWRITING**!

ALL I HAVE TO DO IS FIND THE PERSON WHOSE HANDWRITING MATCHES THIS NOTE!

I'LL NEED A WRITING SAMPLE FROM EVERYONE IN SCHOOL.
THAT'S 600 KIDS!

HOW DO YOU EXPECT TO-?
GIMME.
HEY!
Peirce

WHAT'S UP, SCOOBY DOOFUS?
A **DISCOVERY**, THAT'S WHAT'S UP!

LOOK AT MADELINE RAYBURN'S CIVIL WAR TIMELINE! SEE THAT HANDWRITING? IT MATCHES THE NOTE!

IT LOOKS LIKE **MADELINE'S** THE MYSTERY GIRL WHO THINKS I'M ADORABLE!
BUT MADELINE GOES OUT WITH JOE TARBOX!

SHE'S NOT THE FIRST TO BE TEMPTED BY THE FRUIT OF THE "NATE TREE."
ACTUALLY, YES, SHE IS.
Peirce

AH! MADELINE, MY DEAR! I'VE DISCOVERED YOUR LITTLE "SECRET!"

UH... WHAT?
THIS **NOTE**, OF COURSE! I ONLY READ A **PIECE** OF IT, BUT I DIDN'T **NEED** TO READ MORE!

I BELIEVE THE PART WHERE YOU WROTE "NATE IS ABSOLUTELY ADORABLE" SAYS IT ALL!
! !

HA HA HA HA HA HA
NOT GOOD.
TOLD YA.
Peirce

ate is absolutely
DORABLE!! I hope
HOLD IT, MADELINE! WHAT'S GOING ON?
HA HA HA HA

MY DETECTIVE WORK TOLD ME THAT'S YOUR HANDWRITING!
IT IS.

HA! SO I WAS RIGHT! YOU WROTE THAT NOTE!
YUP!

ABOUT ME.
HA HA HA HA HA HA HA HA HA HA HA HA
Peirce

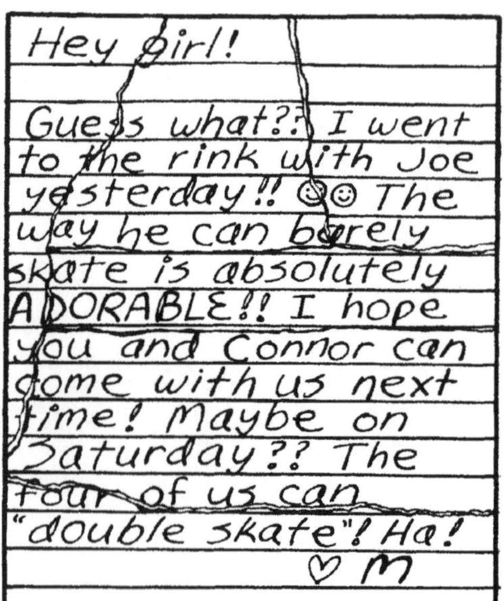

Hey girl!

Guess what?? I went to the rink with Joe yesterday!! ☺☺ The way he can barely skate is absolutely ADORABLE!! I hope you and Connor can come with us next time! Maybe on Saturday?? The four of us can "double skate"! Ha!

♡ M

Big Nate is distributed internationally by Andrews McMeel Syndication.

Andrews McMeel Publishing
a division of Andrews McMeel Universal
1130 Walnut Street, Kansas City, Missouri 64106

www.andrewsmcmeel.com

17 18 19 20 21 SDB 10 9 8 7 6 5 4 3 2 1

ISBN: 978-1-4494-6230-7

Library of Congress Control Number: 2016959642

Made by:
Shenzhen Donnelley Printing Company Ltd.
Address and location of manufacturer:
No. 47, Wuhe Nan Road, Bantian Ind. Zone,
Shenzhen China, 518129
1st Printing—6/5/17

These strips appeared in newspapers from
April 14, 2013, through October 5, 2013, and on May 25, 2014.

Big Nate can be viewed on the Internet at
www.gocomics.com/big_nate

Check out these and other books at ampkids.com

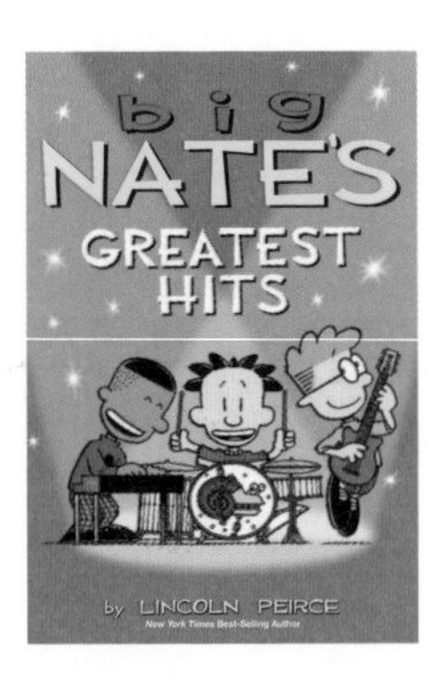

Also available:
Teaching and activity guides for each title.
AMP! Comics for Kids books make reading FUN!